S0-ANF-113

Herbie, the Runaway Duck

by
W.G. Van de Hulst

illustrated by
Willem G. Van de Hulst, Jr.

INHERITANCE PUBLICATIONS
NEERLANDIA, ALBERTA, CANADA
PELLA, IOWA, U.S.A.

Library and Archives Canada Cataloguing in Publication
Hulst, W. G. van de (Willem Gerrit), 1879-1963
[Grote Bertus en kleine Bertus. English]
   Herbie, the runaway duck / by W.G. Van de Hulst ; illustrated
by Willem G. Van de Hulst, Jr. ; [translated by Harry der Nederlanden].
(Stories children love ; 19)
Translation of: Grote Bertus en kleine Bertus.
Originally published: St. Catharines, Ontario : Paideia Press, 1981.
ISBN 978-1-928136-19-4 (pbk.)
   I. Hulst, Willem G. van de (Willem Gerrit), 1917-, illustrator
II. Nederlanden, Harry der, translator III. Title. IV. Title: Grote Bertus
en kleine Bertus.English V. Series: Hulst, W. G. van de (Willem Gerrit),
1879-1963 Stories children love ; 19
PZ7.H873985Her 2014   j839.313'62   C2014-903612-4

Library of Congress Cataloging-in-Publication Data
Hulst, W. G. van de (Willem Gerrit), 1879-1963.
[Grote Bertus en kleine Bertus. English.]
Herbie, the runaway duck / by W.G. Van de Hulst ; illustrated by Willem G. Van de Hulst,
Jr. ; edited by Paulina Janssen.
   pages cm. — (Stories children love ; #19)
"Originally published in Dutch as Grote Bertus en kleine Bertus. Original translation done
by Harry der Nederlanden for Paideia Press, St. Catharines-Ontario-Canada."
Summary: Herbie has a sore knee and a big task to finish, but when a little girl asks for his
help in catching her duckling—also named Herbie—he disobeys his parents and sets out
to help her.
ISBN 978-1-928136-19-4
   [1. Lost and found possessions—Fiction. 2. Friendship—Fiction. 3. Behavior—Fiction.
4. Ducks—Fiction. 5. Animals—Infancy—Fiction. 6. Farm life—Fiction.] I. Hulst,
Willem G. van de (Willem Gerrit), 1917- illustrator. II. Title.
PZ7.H887Her 2014   [E]—dc23   2014017995

Originally published in Dutch as *Grote Bertus en kleine Bertus*
Cover painting and illustrations by Willem G. Van de Hulst, Jr.
Original translation done by Harry der Nederlanden for Paideia Press,
St. Catharines-Ontario-Canada.
The publisher expresses his appreciation to John Hultink of Paideia Press for
his generous permission to use his translation (ISBN 0-88815-519-0).

Edited by Paulina Janssen

ISBN 978-1-928136-19-4

All rights reserved © 2014, by Inheritance Publications
Box 154, Neerlandia, Alberta Canada T0G 1R0
Tel. (780) 674 3949
Web site: www.inhpubl.net
E-Mail inhpubl@telusplanet.net

Published simultaneously in U.S.A. by Inheritance Publications
Box 366, Pella, Iowa 50219

Printed in Canada

Contents

1. The Accident

There once was a little boy.
He lived on a farm.

He had round, rosy cheeks and friendly eyes.
But he was a little shy.

The little boy was sitting at an open window.
All alone.

Father was working in the fields. Mother was in town selling eggs. And the boy had to sort white beans from brown beans. The two kinds of beans were all mixed together. The boy had to sit very still because one of his legs was stiff and sore.

Something had happened to him that morning; something terrible.

That morning he had gone into the pantry for an empty bottle. He had wanted to make himself a bottle of lemonade. But the bottle stood on a high shelf. To reach it, he climbed up on two barrels, one full of white beans and the other full of brown beans.

Then it happened. The barrels tipped over. Hundreds of white and brown beans spilled across the floor. And the boy tumbled to the floor too. The accident gave him a terrible scare. Quickly he scooped up some handfuls of beans and dumped them back into the two small barrels. But since the pantry was very dark, he couldn't see which were white beans and which were brown beans.

Then the boy ran away as fast as he could. Beside the house was a ditch with a plank over it. The narrow plank bridge was a bit wobbly, so running across it was dangerous.

6

But the boy ran anyway. Oh, no! He fell. And both his wooden shoes splashed into the water. But that wasn't the worst of it. One of the boy's knees banged into a sharp stone on the far side of the ditch. He howled in pain and blood ran down his leg into his stocking.

Father ran up.

Mother ran up.

They were both upset.

"Why did you run over the plank, you silly boy?" grumbled Father. "Look at your knee bleed. And there go your wooden shoes — floating down the ditch. Stop your howling. It was your own fault. I think we'll have to take you to the doctor and have your knee sewn up."

Frightened, the boy began to cry even louder. He didn't want anyone sticking a needle into his knee. Over the boy's head, Father winked at Mother. The boy didn't see the wink because his eyes were filled with tears. Then Father hurried off to fish the wooden shoes out of the ditch.

Mother said, "Hush, I'll take care of your knee." In the kitchen she washed the cut and then took out a long strip of white cloth to wind around his knee. She wound it around once, twice, three times — around and around his knee she wound the bandage.

Then she wiped his face and kissed him. His knee was beginning to feel better already. When Father came in, the boy stood up. But he could hardly walk because his leg was stiff from the bandage wound round and round.

"Now you'll have to sit all day," said Father. "Serves you right."

But he could still walk a little: limpety-step, limpety-step.

2. Sorting Beans

Now the boy was sitting at the window, all alone. Before him on the table lay a mountain of beans, some brown, some white. Under the table stood two small barrels — one for the brown beans and one for the white beans.

The boy's fingers went pick — a white one, pick — a brown one; pick, pick. On and on he worked. Pick, pick. Oh, and the day went by so terribly, terribly slow. Pick, pick, pick.

Outside the sun shone. The birds sang and flew in the blue sky. Water shone in the ditch outside the window and the frogs played leap-frog. But the boy had to sit inside picking at the mountain of beans with his  stiff leg stretched out under the table. He looked very sad. He dropped a handful of white beans into the barrel of brown beans. But he was so sad that he didn't even notice.

And it was all his own fault.

The boy's name was Herbie.

On the other side of the ditch were willow woods. People gathered willow shoots to make baskets. Those willow shoots were now covered with thousands of tiny, golden pussies.

The wind, sighing through the window, whispered to the sad little boy. It told him about sweet-smelling flowers and dancing, rustling leaves. It told him many wonderful stories about the woods and it called, "Follow me. Let's play." But Herbie shook his head. "No, my leg is stiff. I can't play."
So the wind rustled on to the woods alone. It played with all those tiny, golden pussy-willows. Their golden fur floated in the air like fluffs of sunshine.

Then came the ducks.
They waddled in single file from the shed beside the house toward the plank. Their short legs and flat feet went flip-flop, flip-flop!

The biggest duck had a
curly tail. He was the father
and he led the way. They
all crossed the plank and
waddled into the woods.
Quack, quack! Quack,
quack!
They called, "Come on.
Follow us over the plank
and into the woods. Quack,
quack!"

But Herbie shook his head. "Over the plank? No,
no, my leg is stiff. I can't play." And his knee
hurt.

Two bright butterflies fluttered by, the sun on their wings. They sat down on the window sill and sang, "Come on, little man, catch us if you can."

Herbie smiled. He forgot the mountain of beans. He forgot his sore leg. He grabbed.

Missed!

Ouch! He banged his sore knee against the table. Oh, that hurt!

The butterflies flitted away, laughing at him. "Come on, little man, catch us if you can."

Herbie sadly shook his head. "No, my leg is stiff. I can't play."

And suddenly he buried his nose in the mountain of beans.

Two big tears trickled down his nose into the beans.

3. The Voice in the Woods

Shh! What was that?

Herbie lifted his head a little. He looked over the mountain of beans and across the ditch. It came from over there, from the woods. Shh! There it was again. Listen! Herbie started in fright.

It was a voice, a high, soft voice calling from the woods.

How could that be? Only frogs and birds and mosquitos lived there. And on the other side of the woods, far away, was a big field. Only cows lived there.

Shh! There it was again.

Herbie's eyes grew wide as he listened. The voice called, "Herbie! He-erbie!" But who . . . who could be calling him? Listen, listen! The voice kept calling, "Herbie, where are you? Come here, you bad boy! Please, Herbie, come back!"

All at once he felt very shy. The voice was calling *him*. But he didn't know whose voice it was. The voice belonged to a stranger. But Herbie did not see anyone in the thick woods. Who was calling him?

Quack, quack, quack!
Oh, look, the ducks were hurrying back out of the woods, running as fast as they could. The father duck was the fastest; he was far out in front. Quack, quack, quack!
They waddled over the plank toward the house. Flip-flap, flip-flap went their frightened feet. Quack! Oh, look, another duck was coming out of the woods — a little duck, a white duckling. He ran too; he ran as fast as his short legs could carry him. But he was so little that he couldn't keep up with the big ducks. Quack!

He stopped at the plank. It frightened him. He flapped his wings. But he was afraid to cross. In a panic, he ran back and forth. He put one foot on the plank and then pulled it back. Quack, quack! Suddenly the pussy-willows behind the duckling trembled.

And then . . .

Oh, at once a foot wearing a brown shoe came out of the willows. Two small hands parted the pussy-willows.

A girl! A little girl stepped out of the willow woods. The sun shone on her hair and made it glisten like gold. On one arm she carried a basket. The basket's lid had a red ribbon on it. When Herbie looked closer, he saw that the little girl's nose was green and that one of her stockings was torn. She looked very sad. Herbie looked through the window and the girl looked through the pussy-willows. They saw each other but they did not know each other.

Herbie blushed. He was a little shy. He ducked behind the mountain of beans but he kept one eye on the girl.

What a strange girl! What a pretty girl!

4. Herbie, the Runaway Duck

"Herbie! He-erbie!"

The boy ducked down even farther.

"Herbie! Come here. Come here right this minute!"

Her high, soft voice was angry. The boy lifted his head from behind the mountain of beans and said, "No, I can't. My leg is stiff. I can't play."

The girl looked at him, eyes wide with surprise.

"No, silly boy, I wasn't calling *you*."

"Yes, you were. My name is Herbie."

"No, you silly boy. I don't want *you*. I'm looking for my little white duckling."

The boy laughed. "Herbie isn't a duck's name," he said.

"It is so!" said the girl. "My papa named him." And she dashed after the little white duckling, trying to catch him.

But little Herbie didn't want to be caught. He ran and hopped and fluttered his wings.

Then he headed for the ditch.

"No, no!" cried the girl.

"No, no!" cried big Herbie. He wanted to help the little girl. "Shoo, shoo!" he shouted from the window. He threw a handful of beans at little Herbie. The frightened duckling stopped and ran the other way.

The girl grabbed for him. Missed! Quick little Herbie darted away in the nick of time.

The girl looked sad and angry.
She *had* to catch her duckling. She just *had* to!
She called to the boy, "Come and help me! I can't catch him by myself. Come on!"
"Me?"
"Yes, you! Hurry, I need you!"
"But my leg is . . ."
"Come on! I'll be your friend. You *have* to help me!"
"But my leg is . . ."
"Please? Won't you come and help me?" Herbie saw tears in her eyes.

Herbie just couldn't say no this time.
When the wind had whispered, "Come on!" he had answered no.
When the ducks had quacked, "Come on, follow us!" he had answered no.
When the butterflies had sung, "Come on, little man, catch us if you can!" he had answered no.

But when the girl cried, "Please come and help me!" he did not answer no.

Clumsily he got up from his chair. As he bumped the table, it rocked and shook the mountain of beans. Beans pitter-pattered to the floor — brown ones and white ones. But Herbie didn't hear or see them fall.

Limpety-step, limpety-step. Off he went.

Oh, that pesky leg, that stiff, pesky leg!

He could hardly walk. Limpety-step, limpety-step. He reached the plank.

Waving at him to come, the girl called, "Come on, hurry!" In the sun her hair looked like gold.

But that plank . . . That wobbly plank . . .

Limpety-step. Oh, the plank wobbled dreadfully. Herbie turned pale with fear. What if he fell in the ditch with his bandaged leg?

The girl saw him and felt sorry for him. What was wrong with his leg? He had a huge bump on his knee.

She said, "Come on, I'll help you." And she held out her hand. He took it. Limpety-shuffle. Yes, it worked! Limpety-shuffle. One more step. Yes, he had made it across the plank.

Just then the pretty white duckling darted back into the woods.

5. The Hollow Willow Tree

"Quack, quack! You'll never catch me. Quack, quack!"
Little Herbie squeezed through the swaying willow shoots. He fluttered across muddy furrows and hid behind a gnarled old willow tree.
The boy and the girl chased him.
"Don't worry, we'll get him," said the girl.
"Yes, we'll get him," said the boy.
Little Herbie was very fast, but big Herbie was moving faster and faster.
Limpety-hop, limpety-hop.

Big Herbie was fast, but the girl was clever. She used her head. "Shh! Shh!" she said. Limping and hopping after the duckling, the boy screamed and shouted. "Shh!" said the girl. "Shh!" She sat down on her heels and put out her hand to tug at Herbie's clothes. But she was looking at the duck, not at Herbie, and she tugged at the big bandage around his leg instead. The bandage began to come loose but she didn't notice. "Shh! Shh!" Foolish little Herbie! He hopped into a hollow tree. "Then they won't see me," he thought and pushed his head into a dark corner. But big Herbie did see him. He tiptoed closer. Limpety-step. The bandage dangled down from his knee. Limpety-step. The girl came after him, a finger pressed to her lips. "Shh!" Her eyes shone with happiness. Only a few more steps. Snatching the girl's basket from her hand, Herbie suddenly jumped forward. He threw himself flat on his stomach and slammed the basket in front of the hole in the willow tree.

"I got you!" he shouted.

"Hold him! Hold him!" cried the girl, jumping up and down with joy. One foot slipped into a mudhole but she did not notice. She threw herself

down on her stomach beside the willow tree and pressed her hands against the basket too. "Hold him! Hold him!"

The duckling was caught.
"Quack, quack! Let me go! Let me go!"
But his quacking did no good. Four hands reached into the hole to grab his head and his legs and his wings. All those hands pulled him out of the hollow tree and held him tightly.
"Quack, quack!" he hollered but it did no good. Little Herbie was caught.

"Let's put him in the basket," said the girl. Her eyes sparkled.
"All right," said big Herbie. "You open the basket. I'll hold the duck."

"Make sure he doesn't get away."
She lifted the lid. Inside the basket lay two small
pieces of bread. The rest of the bread had
bounced out while she was chasing the duckling.
The girl said, "First I'll make a soft little bed in
the basket." But she had nothing soft. She tried
putting her handkerchief in the bottom of the
basket but it was much too small. Then her eyes
fell on something else. Yes, that would be
perfect!
She had noticed the bandage trailing from big
Herbie's leg. Grabbing the end of it she pulled
— and almost knocked Herbie over.
"Is that all right?" she asked.

"Sure, that's all right," he answered cheerfully.
Rrrip! The girl tore a long piece from the bandage.
That would make a bed for little Herbie.
"Quick, put him in. Don't let him get away."
The boy stuffed the duckling into the basket.
Thump! They slammed the lid shut. Little Herbie
was trapped in the basket at last.

6. Eggs or Bacon?

Big Herbie and the girl sat side by side in the
woods. They had found a pool of water and were
carefully cleaning the girl's muddy shoes.
The girl was sitting on her knees. Herbie sat on
only one knee because his other one was stiff

and sore. The basket stood alone between the golden pussy-willows.

The girl said, "It's funny that my duckling has the same name as you."

The boy said, "Ducks don't have names."

"They do so!"

"No, they don't!"

"They do so! My papa gave him to me and he said his name is Herbie. And my papa knows everything. He's a doctor."

A doctor? The boy shuddered. He looked down at his knee. It ached. His father had told him not to walk on it or else he'd have to go to the doctor.

"Does your father stick needles in knees?"

"I don't know, but my duck's name is *so* Herbie. And my mama is gone. She went to the city to visit Grandma because Grandma is sick. So I had to bring some bread to Herbie in our back yard. We have a big backyard with a pond in it. But when I got there, Herbie was gone. He had squeezed through the hedge and was walking way out in the field on the other side. So I squeezed through the hedge too. I ran very fast. I ran so fast I fell on my nose. That hurt!"

"Yes, and your nose is green."

"Green? From the grass?"

She wiped her nose with her handkerchief.

"Is it clean now?"

"No, it's still green."

"You do it."

Herbie said, "I'll dip the handkerchief in the water. That will do it."

He rubbed and he rubbed.

The girl said, "Ouch, you're hurting me! Is my nose still green?"

"No," said Herbie. "Just a little black."

"Oh, you're silly! Give me that handkerchief!"

The basket stood all alone between the golden pussy-willows.

Squeak! The lid of the basket moved. A little duckbill peeped out through the crack.

But the boy and the girl did not see it.

"Oh, and then my duckling saw a whole bunch of big ducks out in the field."

"Those were ours."

"Yes, and then he followed them into the woods . . . What happened to your knee?"

"I hurt it when I fell on the plank across the ditch."

"I'm sure my papa could fix it."

"Oh, no, it's all right. My mother fixed it."

"Do you know my name?"

"No."

"My name is Elly."

"Elly? What a funny name!"

"It is not! It's a nice name. I think Herbie is a funny name."

"But your duck's name is Herbie too."

Squeak! The lid on the basket moved again.
A little white head peeked out through the crack.
But the boy and the girl did not see it.

27

"Why don't you ask *your* papa to get you a duckling?"

"My father isn't called Papa; he's called Father."

"Do you think he would give you a duckling?"

"Maybe. And then I'll sell the eggs like my mother does."

"Oh, yes, so will I. When my duck lays eggs, I will sell them too."

"Good," said Herbie. "We'll go to town together. Just like my mother."

"Yes!" cried Elly. "I have an idea, a wonderful idea." Elly was so excited that she danced around the little pool on one foot.

Squeak! The lid on the basket moved again.
A soft, white body wriggled through the crack.
Then came two orange legs. Flip-flap, flip-flap. The lid fell shut. Thump!
But the boy and the girl did not notice anything.

"I know! We'll get married and have a duck farm."

"Yes," said Herbie.

"We'll have a big house and a big pond and lots and lots of ducks. And the ducks will lay millions of eggs. And . . ."

"Yes," said Herbie.

"And then we'll make lots of pancakes. I love pancakes, pancakes with eggs."

"No, you don't," said Herbie. "Pancakes with eggs, no! You eat them with bacon."

"You do not! With eggs!"

"With bacon!"

"My mama always makes pancakes with eggs. Thin ones. That's how you make them."

"But *my* mother always makes them with bacon. Real thick ones. *That's* how you make them."

"Not me!"

"You have to!"

"I do not! Then I won't marry you!"

Angrily Elly put on her wet shoe.

Herbie said, "And I won't marry you!"

"I'm not your friend anymore!" said Elly. She picked up her basket. Without looking into it she marched away, her little black nose high in the air.

Herbie was left alone. "You do so make pancakes with bacon!" he called.

Elly walked on between the golden pussy-willows and disappeared.

Herbie thought, "I had better get back home and finish sorting beans."
Quickly he limped toward home. Limpety-step, limpety-step. A long strip of bandage dragged along behind him.

7. Herbie the Brave

"Herbie! Herbie! Oh, help! Help!"
Herbie stopped short and looked back, startled. It was Elly. She was pushing her way back through the golden pussy-willows. She cried, "I'm scared, Herbie!" She looked at him with huge, frightened eyes.

"What's the matter?" he asked. She made him scared too.

"A cow. A big ugly cow. It's standing in the field on the other side of the bushes. I'm afraid to go past it. It has such big horns!"

Even with his sore knee, Herbie was a brave little boy.

"Just follow me," he said. "There's nothing to be afraid of."

Together they pushed through the pussy-willows until they reached the field. There it stood: a big, fat cow with curved horns. It stared and stared at them.

But Herbie was very brave. "Come on," he said. "Just follow me." And he limped ahead. Limpety-step, limpety-step.

Elly tiptoed along behind him, trembling with fear. They had to pass close to the big cow. How that cow stared! Elly put out her hand to grab Herbie's shirt. But she missed because he was walking too fast. He was so brave!

Looking for something to hold onto, Elly saw the bandage dragging along after Herbie. Grabbing it, she tried to hide behind him so that the cow wouldn't see her.

Oh, oh . . . they were getting so close . . .

Suddenly Herbie shouted, "Yaaa!" waving his
arms wildly and hopping around on his good leg.
"Yaaa, yaaa!"

The shouting and waving frightened the cow. It
jumped sideways, rolled its eyes, and ran off,
its tail sticking straight up in the air. The ground
shook as it ran.

"Come on, hurry! Follow me," said Herbie. He
limped ahead very fast. Limpety-step, limpety-
step, limpety-step.

Elly ran along behind him, clutching the long
bandage that was coming unwound from Herbie's
knee. The basket with its red ribbon bobbed
along on her arm. Ahead was the hedge and on

the other side of it there was a big yard and the big house where Elly lived.

Yes — but . . .
But, on the other side of the hedge . . .
Someone was standing there.
Someone with glasses . . . He waved his hand angrily and shouted, "Come here, Elly! You naughty girl, where have you been? I've been looking all over for you."
Elly shouted, "I'm coming, Papa! Herbie got away, but I caught him. He's in the basket. This boy helped me. And his name is Herbie too. He's very brave, Papa! Come on, Herbie, you can come."
She tried to pull him along by the bandage around his knee.

But Herbie had stopped and he wouldn't move.
His face turned red and his breath came fast.
That man was the doctor and he looked angry. He sounded angry too. Look, was he waving at Elly to hurry up or was he shaking his fist at him? Herbie shuddered. Then, tugging the bandage from Elly's hand, he turned and hopped off as fast as he could go. Limpety-hop, limpety-hop.

Elly came to the hedge all alone. Her father lifted her over. Angrily he scolded, "You naughty girl! You should not run off without telling us. Look at you: your nose is black, your stocking is torn, and your shoes are wet."

"But I've got him, Papa! I got Herbie back. Do you want me to show you? He's in the basket." She crouched beside the basket. Very slowly, very carefully, she opened the lid.

Oh, inside the basket lay a dirty piece of white bandage. And that was all.

8. Poor Herbie!

Poor Herbie! Poor big Herbie!
When he got home his father was very angry. He said, "You were a bad boy. I told you not to walk on your sore leg but you didn't listen. You should have called me. I wasn't very far away. I could have caught the duckling for that little girl. Because you didn't listen, you'll go to bed early tonight."
Mother was also angry. When she came home from the market she said, "You were a bad boy. I told you to sort beans but you ran off. Sit down and get to work. I want all the white beans in this barrel and all the brown beans in this one. Because you didn't listen, you'll go to bed early tonight."

Poor Herbie! It wasn't even dark yet but he had to go to bed.
But — Mother went with him up the stairs. Herbie knelt with his hands on Mother's lap. Softly, reverently he said his bedtime prayer. Mother listened. The Lord in heaven listened too. Then Mother took Herbie in her arms and kissed him good night. She still loved Herbie. And so did Father.

Poor Herbie? No, Herbie was really very rich, for he had a father and mother who loved him.

Clever Herbie! Clever little Herbie.
He had slipped out of the basket without being seen. Then he was free, free to go and do as he pleased. He explored all sorts of wonderful places, looking for good things to eat.
But he found none.
He was all alone.
And there was no one to care for him.
And night was coming.
It was growing dark.
Where would he go? Where would he find a warm nest in the dark night?
Who would protect him from hungry animals looking for a plump little duckling?
What if a big rat or a dog or a fox caught him?
Clever little Herbie? No, little Herbie was a poor, lonely duckling.

9. Herbie in Bed

Night had come. The moon shone down on the water in the ditch. Big Herbie was walking along the ditch looking for something. His leg! He had lost his leg. Oh! Tears streamed down his cheeks.

And then, oh, suddenly a big, fat cow was after him, its head low and its horns jabbing forward. Terrified, Herbie hopped away as fast as he could on one leg. He reached the plank across the ditch. His mouth opened to scream for help but not a sound came out. He hopped and hopped.

Oh, no! He was toppling off the plank into the water. Splash!

And then . . . then Herbie awoke.

Oh, what a relief!

He felt his legs. One . . . two! He still had both of them!

Splish-splash!

Listen! What was that? His window stood open.

Splish-splash!

The splashing was coming from the ditch.

What could it be? The ducks were all sleeping in the shed. Herbie slipped out of bed and looked out the window.

Oh, look! A white duckling was splashing in the ditch. The moon shone on its feathers and made them look as white as snow. Was that . . . could it be little Herbie? But how? Yes, it sure looked like him. Had he slipped away from the little girl again? What if a big rat came along? Or a fox?

"Father! Mother!"

Father and Mother had not gone to bed yet. They were sitting downstairs in the living room. When Herbie called they jumped.

"Father! Mother! Herbie is swimming in the ditch!"

Mother hurried upstairs. "Silly boy!" she said. "You're not swimming in the ditch; you're swimming in bed. You must be dreaming."

"No, Mother, I'm not. It's *little* Herbie. Elly's duckling. We've got to catch him!"

Father went out to the ditch while Herbie and Mother watched from the upstairs window. Father caught him easily. Little Herbie was terribly frightened and tired.

Father walked back into the house carrying the frightened duckling in his cap.

Then he came upstairs to show little Herbie to big Herbie. He said, "Well, Mother, you put big

Herbie to bed and I'll put little Herbie to bed."
Mother tucked big Herbie under the blankets and
Father put little Herbie in the warm shed with
the other ducks.

Then they both had a safe warm place to sleep.
Good night!

10. The Doctor's House

The next morning Herbie was off. He did not go
across the plank. He did not go through the
woods. He followed the road.

The sun shone but Herbie wore his beautiful knit
cap. It sat a little crooked on his head. Mother
had scrubbed his wooden shoes bright and white.
Under his arm Herbie carried a small basket
which he held tightly. The lid was tied shut with
a sturdy piece of rope.

Herbie walked fast, taking long steps. He thought, "Won't Elly be happy! I guess Elly isn't such a funny name after all."

Mother had not wrapped a new bandage around his knee and he no longer walked limpety-step.

Ahead was the doctor's big house with its shiny door. Herbie slowed down. Beside the door a large window stood wide open. Would the doctor be home? Herbie slowed down even more. Beside the house was a wide yard surrounded by a tall iron fence. Oh, Herbie had a sudden idea. Yes, that was what he would do! Herbie stuck his head through the gate and looked this way and that. Elly wasn't in the yard. Maybe if he called her she would come. "Elly! Elly!" he called softly. "I've got him again. I've got little Herbie."

No one answered. No one came.

He would have to call louder.

"Elly! Where are you? El-l-ly!"

Oh, no!

Suddenly a head popped out of a window. A voice said, "Who are you? What are you doing here?"

Oh, no! It was the doctor, the stern, gruff doctor. Herbie jerked back his head. His heart hammered wildly. He pulled his knit cap off his head and

40

held it over his scraped knee. He didn't want
the doctor to see it.

"What do you want?" asked the doctor. "Come
over here."

Trembling, Herbie stepped a little closer. The doctor looked so stern that Herbie did not dare to disobey him.

Oh, and then . . .

The doctor looked at him. "Did you hurt your knee? Let me take a look at it."

"No! No!"cried Herbie. He was so scared that he began to cry.

"What a strange boy you are! What are you afraid of? Why are you crying?"

Herbie sobbed, "I don't want you to stick a needle in my knee."

"Stick a needle in your knee? Oh, you mean stitches!" The doctor threw back his head and laughed. "You silly boy, that's only a scrape."

Suddenly another head appeared in the window — a small head with beautiful hair. The sun shone on it and made it glisten like gold. There was Elly; she was standing on a chair.

"Hello, Herbie! *Herbie* is gone again."

Herbie looked up at her through his tears. "No, he isn't."

"Yes, he is!"

"No, he isn't. I've got him."

"You have? Where is he?"

"Here, in my basket."

Quickly Herbie untied the rope and lifted the lid — just a little. A small, yellow bill peeped out through the crack.

"Oh, Papa, it *is* Herbie! Herbie's back!"

Elly was so happy that she threw her arms around her father's neck and kissed him.

The doctor laughed. "Hey, *I* didn't find Herbie. That boy did. Hurry outside and you can both bring that little runaway back to his pond."

Together Herbie and Elly walked through the huge yard carrying the basket between them. The doctor followed them bringing a bowl full of pieces of bread.

Splash! Little Herbie was again swimming in his own pond. Around the pond was a low fence of chicken wire. The doctor checked it to make sure there weren't any holes along the bottom. No, Herbie couldn't run away again.

Elly threw some pieces of bread into the water but little Herbie didn't look at them. He just paddled sadly around the pond.

The doctor said, "Herbie is lonely. He doesn't like to be alone. He ran away to look for friends. I'll buy another duckling."

"Oh, yes, Papa, yes! Another duckling!" Elly jumped for joy. "I already know what I'm going to call it. I'll call it Elly."

She took big Herbie by the hand and pulled him along after her. "When we play house, I'll be the mommy and you'll be the daddy and little Herbie and little Elly will be our children. Won't that be fun?"

Herbie just smiled.

"And we'll make pancakes — pancakes with eggs. I'm not making pancakes with bacon."

Herbie blushed and didn't say anything. He was afraid to argue.

Then Elly said, "I'll tell you what. When it's your birthday we'll make pancakes with bacon. All right?"

"All right," said Herbie.

The doctor bit his lip to keep from laughing. He said, "I have an idea. Just follow me — both of you."

11. Vroom

In front of the house stood the doctor's car.
The doctor said, "Hop in. First the bride and then
the groom."
Then he stepped in himself and sat down behind
the steering wheel.
Vrrroom! Away they went. The doctor had to
make some house calls. Elly and Herbie were
going along for the ride and afterwards the doctor
would bring Herbie home.
Oh, it was so much fun! Elly and Herbie were
having a great time. Elly said, "Let's pretend
we're the king and the queen out for a ride. We
must act very dignified."
Elly proudly held her nose high in the air.
Herbie thought, "Act dignified? How do you do
that?" He looked at Elly and also held his nose
high in the air. But he didn't look dignified at
all. His knit cap slid down over one eye.
Elly giggled.
As the doctor turned a corner, the king and queen
both tumbled into a corner of the back seat.
Vrrroom!

Toot-toot!
It was a long, wonderful ride, but at last the big

car stopped in front of Herbie's house.

Mother was standing outside hanging out the wash. Father was in the garden planting potatoes. First they saw the beautiful car drive up. And then they saw Herbie in the back seat, his knit cap down over one eye.

Mother quickly straightened her hair. Father wiped his dirty hands on his pants. They both walked toward the gate.

The doctor lifted Herbie from the car and said, "You have quite a boy here. Elly has invited him to come over tomorrow. Is that all right?"

"Yes, of course, doctor," said Mother.

"Yes, sir," said Father.

"Good. Now Elly and I are going to the city to pick up her mother. We'll see you tomorrow, Herbie."

Elly said, "Maybe my mama will let us make real pancakes. Papa is going to ask her."

The doctor said, "Well, Elly, who do you like the most — big Herbie or little Herbie?"

"I like them both just as much," said Elly.
"Maybe I like big Herbie just a tiny bit more."
The doctor laughed. "Yes, I thought so. But if
little Herbie hadn't run away, you'd never have
met big Herbie. Good-bye!"

Vrrroom!
Away they drove. Elly knelt on the backseat,
looking back. "Good-bye!" she cried. "See you
tomorrow!"
Herbie stood on the road waving his cap with
one hand and his basket with the other. "Good-
bye!" he cried. "See you tomorrow!"
The car disappeared around the corner. Too bad.
But tomorrow he would see Elly again. She was
nice. And pancakes with eggs would be just fine.

Titles in this series:

1. The Little Wooden Shoe
2. Through the Thunderstorm
3. Bruno the Bear
4. The Basket
5. Lost in the Snow
6. Annie and the Goat
7. The Black Kitten
8. The Woods beyond the Wall
9. My Master and I
10. The Pig under the Pew
11. Three Little Hunters
12. The Search for Christmas
13. Footprints in the Snow
14. Little Tramp
15. Three Foolish Sisters
16. The Secret Hiding Place
17. The Secret in the Box
18. The Rockity Rowboat
19. Herbie, the Runaway Duck
20. Kittens, Kittens Everywhere
21. The Forbidden Path